Kaml

Illustrated by Thelma Lambert

Kamla and Kate are the very best of friends. They learn about each other's way of life, and together they get up to all kinds of mischief – such as covering Kamla's bedroom wall with potato prints!

Kamla and Kate

JAMILA GAVIN

MAMMOTH

First published in Great Britain 1983
by Methuen Children's Books Ltd
Paperback edition published 1986 by Magnet
Reissued 1991 by Mammoth
an imprint of Mandarin paperbacks
Michelin House, 81 Fulham Road, London SW3 6RB

Mandarin is an imprint of the Octopus Publishing Group

Text copyright © 1983 Jamila Gavin
Illustrations copyright © 1983 Thelma Lambert

ISBN 0 7497 0581 7

A CIP catalogue record for this title
is available from the British Library

Printed in Great Britain
by Cox and Wyman Ltd, Reading, Berkshire

Contents

1

Hello Kamla! Hello Kate!

Kate swung on her garden gate. She was bored and cross because she had no one to play with. Plenty of children lived in her street, but they were all boys and playing with boys all the time could be very boring.

It's true that Mrs. Grant up the road had had a baby girl the other day, but there wasn't much you could do with a baby, and she would take ages to grow up.

Suddenly, Kate noticed a huge removal van draw up outside Number 82. The house had been empty for ages, and the gardens at the front and back had become quite wild. Some naughty children had discovered a hole in the fence and sneaked through after dark to steal apples, and collect the blackberries which trailed across the over-grown lawn.

It had seemed as though the house would stay empty for ever and just be a forbidden playground for mischievous boys and girls. The 'For Sale' notice which had stood in front for ages had fallen down long ago, and no 'Sold' board had ever come up in its place.

Kate stopped swinging on the gate and walked out on to the pavement. She began to feel excited. Was a new family moving in at last?

She hopped and skipped down the road until she reached the removal van. Two men in brown overalls had opened up the back and were somewhere inside shifting things around.

Kate peered inside and was amazed at what she saw. It was like looking inside a huge house. The van was full of furniture; there were tables and chairs, cupboards and book-cases, a wardrobe and dressing table, beds and a sofa, rolls of carpets, and lots and lots of wooden crates.

But where were the people who were going to live in the house?

Then she noticed a small, red car parked just a little way down the road. A tall, dark man had got out and was walking up to Number 82, fumbling in his pockets for the keys. He waved at the removal men and opened the front door.

A moment later, a lady with shining, black hair coiled in a bun got out of the car. She seemed to tinkle and glitter as she straightened up. Kate saw that it was the bangles on her arms which tinkled, and the gold of her earrings and necklace which glittered in the sun. She was wearing something long and colourful underneath a brown coat, and Kate realised it was a saree.

The lady bent into the car and brought out a tiny bundle of a baby. Kate held her breath and waited. Would anyone else get out? She could not get a clear view inside the car as it was so crammed with bags and parcels and odds and ends.

The lady walked away towards the house, and Kate was just about to give up with disappointment and go home, when suddenly there was another movement.

First a leg in jeans appeared, then a hand, then a bit of dark hair, and then a whole body. Then Kate jumped with delight. It was a girl.

For a few moments the two girls stared at each other. It was a bit like looking in a mirror, for although one was very dark and one was very fair, they were both the same height and wearing jeans; they both had green tee-shirts and they were both wearing identical green and white canvas shoes.

The lady in the saree stood at the front door of Number 82 and called out to her daughter in a language Kate couldn't understand. The girl replied in the same language but didn't stop staring at Kate.

'Oh dear!' thought Kate. 'They don't speak English.' But suddenly the girl said, 'Hello!'

'Hello!' replied Kate shyly. 'What was that language you were talking to your Mum?'

'That was Hindi,' laughed the girl.

'Can you really understand that?' cried Kate. 'It sounds Double Dutch to me.'

'Of course I can,' said the girl. 'What's your name?'

'Kate,' said Kate. 'What's yours?'

'Kamla,' said the girl. 'How old are you?'

'I'm six,' said Kate.

'I'm six too,' cried Kamla.

'Are you going to my school?' asked Kate. 'I expect we'll be in the same class. We can be friends,' she said excitedly.

'I may not like you,' replied Kamla.

'Well then, you'll have to play with the boys after school,' said Kate huffily. 'I'm the only girl in the road.'

'Well, I don't know if I'm going to your school, and anyway I must go now and help carry in our things.' And with that Kamla ran over to her new house and disappeared into the long weeds.

Kate ran home to tell her mother. 'I may have a new friend,' she told her, 'but she doesn't know if she likes me yet.'

'Who?' asked Mum.

'Kamla,' said Kate. 'She's moving into Number 82. She speaks Hindi to her mother. I wish we had our own language to speak to each other that no one else could understand.'

Kate's mother laughed. 'I have enough trouble making myself understood in one language, let alone two! But I do hope Kamla will be your friend, and it will be nice for you to have another girl to play with.'

Kate went back to swinging on the gate. She watched the removal men heaving and pushing the big, heavy bits of furniture into the house, and she watched Kamla and her mother and father trooping to and fro carrying armfuls of smaller things.

Suddenly, Kate noticed Paul Tanner and Gary Fisher creeping into the garden of Number 82. When they thought no one was looking, they dashed into the long grass and lay hidden on their tummies.

Paul and Gary were always up to mischief. They were probably playing at spying on Kamla and her family. Kate decided to tell Kamla. She wandered down the road,

13

pretending not to see the boys, then caught Kamla as she came out of the house and whispered in her ear.

'Let's give them a fright,' she hissed.

'Follow me,' said Kamla, and she took Kate into the house.

Everything was bare inside the house. Their footsteps echoed on the bare floor boards, and Kate wondered how they would ever make this house look like home.

Kamla took her through to the kitchen at the back of the house.

'Let's go out of the kitchen door and creep up the side of the house.'

'Yes!' agreed Kate, 'and then we'll jump on them!'

The two girls crept silently along the alley until they could see Paul and Gary crouching with their backs to them. Then Kate gave the signal, and the girls ran screaming towards the boys, waving their arms.

Everyone stopped and looked round.

'What's going on?' asked the removal men.

'What's going on?' asked Kamla's mother and father.

But Gary and Paul didn't stop to find out.

14

They took to their heels and ran while Kamla and Kate roared with laughter.

Just then Kate's mother came over to ask if the newcomers would like a cup of tea.

'That's very kind of you,' said Kamla's father. 'We'd like one very much.'

Kamla looked at Kate and Kate looked at Kamla.

'Have you noticed we're wearing the same clothes?' asked Kate.

'Yes,' replied Kamla, 'we could be sisters.'

'That's what I thought,' said Kate, 'we can at least be friends.'

2
Kamla and Kate are Friends

On Monday morning Kate set off for school with her mother. As they passed Number 82 they could see that already it was beginning to look like home. There were bright curtains in the windows, and the long grass had been cut away from the path leading to the front door.

Just then, the door opened and Kamla and her mother stepped out.

'Hello Kamla!' called Kate.

'Hello Kate!' called Kamla.

'I hope we're still friends today,' Kate whispered to her mother, as Kamla and her mother came down the path.

'We can all walk to school together,' said Kate's mother smiling at Kamla's mother. Kamla's mother didn't speak English, so she just smiled back and nodded shyly.

'You're coming to my school,' said Kate. 'Your Dad told my Dad.'

'Yes, I know,' replied Kamla. 'I'm glad.'

They walked happily along together until they reached the school railings. Kate said goodbye to her mother at the gate, but because Kamla was new, she and her mother walked together down the path to the school. Kate was so excited at having a new friend that she hopped around them like a sparrow, sometimes skipping in front, sometimes dropping behind.

Kamla came into the classroom holding her mother's hand tightly. Suddenly she didn't want to come to school anymore and she looked as if she might cry. But Mrs. Stevens, their teacher, came and gave Kamla a hug and said, 'Don't worry, dear, you'll have a lovely time at school. As you and Kate live in the same road I'm sure Kate will look after you.'

'Oh yes!' cried Kate. 'We're already friends.'

'Then you had better sit at the same table and you can tell Kamla all she needs to know about school,' said Mrs. Stevens with a smile.

Kate looked after Kamla all day. She showed her everything; the toilets and wash-rooms, the hall for assembly and P.E., the lockers under the pegs where they kept their gym shoes and tee-shirts, but most of all she showed her all the good places to play in the playground.

When school was over, Kate and Kamla came out holding hands. They walked together up to the school railings at the top where their mothers were waiting for them.

'Kamla is my best friend,' Kate told her mother proudly.

Kamla hugged her mother and pointed to Kate. 'She is my friend!' she shouted happily.

The two mothers looked at each other and smiled. Perhaps they could be friends too, but it is hard when you don't speak the same language.

'Kamla! You must teach your mother to speak English so that she and I can be friends too!' said Kate's mum.

'Please can Kamla come to tea today?' begged Kate.

Her mother nodded. 'Yes, of course, if Kamla's mother lets her.'

Kamla beamed with delight. She tugged her mother's saree and spoke to her in her own language. Her mother looked pleased and said in English, 'Yes. Thank you.'

'Mummy says yes! Mummy says yes!' shouted Kamla with glee, 'and she'll come and get me at six o'clock!'

The two mothers smiled at each other and they all set off for home.

'You are clever being able to speak two languages like that, Kamla!' said Kate's mother. 'I can only speak one – English! But if I try and help your mother to speak English, perhaps I can learn a few words of Hindi!'

When they reached Number 82, Kamla's mother waved goodbye and went in to feed the baby. The others walked on until they came to Number 64, Kate's house.

Kate's mother opened the door. Kamla was the first to rush inside. She ran down the hall and back again to the front door.

'This house has a funny smell,' she said sniffing the air like a puppy dog.

Then Kamla ran into every room sniffing. 'This room smells funny,' she cried in the living room. 'This room smells funny!' she cried in the dining room. 'I don't like this smell,' she said screwing up her nose in the kitchen where Kate's mother had left some sausages slowly cooking in the oven. Kamla even ran upstairs sniffing all over the house, while Kate and her mother looked on laughing.

At last Kamla stopped rushing round sniffing and said, 'Your house doesn't smell like mine.'

'Oh, stop sniffing and come and play!' cried

Kate, and she took Kamla upstairs to her room.

When Kamla saw all Kate's toys and games, she forgot all about the smells. First they played snakes and ladders and then beggar-my-neighbour. Soon their laughter rang through the house. Kate's mother smiled to herself as she made the tea. She was so pleased that at last Kate had a friend in the same road.

Every now and then Kamla and Kate stopped playing and looked at each other. There seemed to be so many things they both liked, and yet they were so different too.

'You've got earrings in your ears,' said Kate looking at Kamla's ears closely. 'How do you put them on?'

'My ears are pierced,' said Kamla, twisting the earring round and round.

'Do you mean you have holes in your ears?' asked Kate, looking shocked.

'Yes, look!' said Kamla and she slipped one of the earrings off. Now Kate could see a tiny hole in Kamla's ear.

'Doesn't it hurt?' asked Kate warily.

'Not at all!' said Kamla. 'My ears were

pierced when I was very little so I'm used to it.'

'My mother wears earrings but she clips them on. Sometimes they hurt her and then she takes them off and loses them,' said Kate with a sigh. 'Perhaps she ought to have her ears pierced!'

'Tea's ready!' called Kate's mother from downstairs.

The two girls rushed downstairs like wild elephants and flopped down on the bench at the kitchen table.

'I'm starving!' cried Kate.

'I'm starving!' cried Kamla.

'Help yourselves then,' said Kate's mother.

Kate immediately helped herself to three sausages.

'Hold on, Kate!' said her mother. 'Look after Kamla first – she's your guest!'

'Have some sausages, Kamla!' said Kate pushing the plate of sausages over to her. Kamla sniffed and wriggled her nose, but

23

didn't move. 'I don't like the smell,' she said.

'What about a few chips, then?' asked Kate's mother anxiously, 'or how about a sandwich?'

Kamla shook her head. 'I don't like the smell of chips or sandwiches,' she said. 'I like chapattis.'

'What are chapattis?' asked Kate.

'Chapattis are chapattis,' replied Kamla.

'Chapattis are Indian bread,' explained Kate's mother. 'Daddy and I love eating them when we have a curry at the Indian restaurant. I'm sorry, Kamla, I don't know how to make them. Perhaps your mother can teach me one day. But what will you eat now?' she asked desperately. 'I can't send you home with an empty tummy.'

Kamla looked at the plate with the chocolate biscuits. She sniffed hard and pointed to them. 'Mmmm,' she said, 'I like the smell of those.'

Kate wasn't too pleased when Kamla was allowed to eat four chocolate biscuits one after the other, and by the time she was ready to eat one there were only two left!

24

After tea the two friends went back to their games, and played until Kamla's mother came to fetch her at six o'clock.

'Thank you for having me,' said Kamla politely. Then just as she was about to leave, she sniffed the air once more.

'I think I do like this smell,' she said.

'Good,' smiled Kate's mother. 'Then do come back to tea again soon.'

3
Potato Trouble

One day, Kamla and Kate went to school
with a potato in their pockets. Mrs. Stevens
had asked every child to bring a potato to
school so they could do potato printing.

First she cut a potato in half, and scraped
out a pattern. Then she let the children
scrape out their own patterns. Kate scraped
out a triangle and Kamla scraped out a
cross.

Then Mrs. Stevens put out a saucer of paint
on each table and handed out sheets of paper.
The children dipped their potatoes into the
paint and pressed them down on to the paper
to make patterns.

Stamp! Stamp! Stamp!

'Look at mine!' cried Kamla excitedly, as
she prodded her potato print down all over
the page, until it was completely filled with
blue crosses.

Do you like my yellow triangles?' cried Kate. 'Why don't we swap colours now? I'm bored with blue.'

'Let's swap potatoes, too,' suggested Kamla, 'I'm bored with crosses.' So they swapped, and Kate printed blue crosses over yellow triangles, and Kamla printed yellow triangles over blue crosses.

Mrs. Stevens was very pleased when she saw what Kamla and Kate had done. She held up their prints to show to the whole class, and later she pinned them up on the wall.

When it was going home time, Mrs. Stevens allowed the children to take their potatoes home. That gave Kamla an idea.

'Come home to tea with me today,' she said, 'and we can do some more potato printing. I've got a new painting set which I had for my birthday. It has lots of pots of different coloured paints. We can make more prints – lots more! Shall we, Kate?'

'Yes, lets!' laughed Kate happily.

After school, the girls and their mothers walked home together.

When they reached Number 82, Kate

waved goodbye to her mother and went into Kamla's house. As she stepped inside the front door, she screwed up her nose.

'Your house smells funny,' she said.

Kamla's mother went into the kitchen to prepare the tea, and Kamla rushed Kate upstairs to her room.

'Look at my paints,' she said, lifting down a box from one of the shelves. She opened the lid, and there were two rows of small pots with all the colours of the rainbow.

'We can make much better prints at home than we did at school,' said Kamla, lifting out the little pots and rushing off to find two saucers.

When she came back, Kate said, 'What about the paper?'

'Let's tear these sheets out of my scrap book,' suggested Kamla and she began ripping them out.

'My favourite colour is red,' said Kate, tipping up the pot of red paint. It flowed out with a great whooosh on to the saucer.

'Whoops! I poured too much!' she said with a giggle.

'I like green,' said Kamla, tipping up the

28

green pot. There was another great whoosh on to the saucer.

'Whoops! I poured too much too,' she giggled.

Then they got their potatoes and began to print. Stamp, stamp, stamp! Soon the whole of one side of paper was filled up and then the other. Kamla tore out more sheets of paper from her scrap book and they filled those up too. They swapped potatoes back and forth. Soon the red paint began to get green in it and the green paint began to get red in it, and their patterns became all purply.

'Let's change colours now!' cried Kamla, getting out the orange pot.

'I'd like the pink paint!' cried Kate.

Stamp, stamp, stamp! They went on printing until they had no more paper left. 'Oh, Kate, just look at your fingers and look at your face!' shrieked Kamla.

'Oh, Kamla! You look just like a clown,' laughed Kate.

The two girls stood giggling in front of the mirror, looking at the blotches of red, green, orange and pink which had got on their cheeks and chins and noses.

'Come on! Let's get back to printing,' said Kamla.

'But there's no more paper left in the scrap book!' said Kate.

Kamla searched her room for more paper, but couldn't find any. Then she stopped and beamed all over her face.

'I've got a good idea. Let's print on my walls. Mummy says I've got to have new wallpaper one of these days, and I hate this wallpaper. Our prints will make it look better.'

'Do you think we should?' asked Kate anxiously.

'Of course,' cried Kamla. 'It's my room anyway.'

So the two girls set to work printing triangles and crosses all over the walls of Kamla's room. Soon they had finished all the green paint and the red paint; all the orange paint and the pink paint; all the pots of blue and violet, yellow and brown, until there was no paint left in any of the jars.

Downstairs in the kitchen, Kamla's mother had finished feeding the baby and preparing tea for the girls. Suddenly she realised how quiet everything was, and she went to the bottom of the stairs. She couldn't hear any chatting or giggling. There was a strange silence. Things were too quiet, and that usually meant trouble.

She hurried upstairs calling, 'Kamla! Kamla!' Then she opened Kamla's bedroom door and gave a shriek of horror.

Kate didn't understand what Kamla's mother said to her daughter, or what Kamla said back to her mother, but she knew that they should not have done potato printing

31

over the bedroom walls, even if Kamla didn't like the wallpaper.

The two girls dropped their heads and Kamla started to cry. But although Kamla's mother was very angry, she did not forget that

Kate was a visitor. She told Kamla to take Kate to the bathroom and get cleaned up. Then even she was able to see the funny side, and had to laugh at the sight of their two painted faces.

Kate and Kamla scrubbed their fingers and faces and rushed down for tea.

'I'm starving,' cried Kamla.

'I'm starving!' cried Kate.

'I told Mummy that you liked sausages and potatoes,' said Kamla. 'Go on! Help yourself,' she urged.

But Kate sat absolutely still and sniffed. 'I don't like the smell,' she said.

Kamla's mother came in and saw that Kate was not eating. 'Eat!' she said in English. 'Eat! Eat!'

'I thought you liked sausages,' said Kamla disappointed.

'These aren't the same as my Mum buys,' said Kate.

Kamla's mother pushed some potatoes in front of Kate. 'Eat! Potato!' she said.

But Kate looked at the curried potato, and sniffed the steam which rose from them and said, 'I don't like potatoes like that.'

Kamla's mother spoke to Kamla, and Kamla explained to Kate. 'Mummy says you can eat anything you like which you can see.'

Kate looked at every plate; the spicy sausages, the curried potato; the napkin of hot chapattis – and the plate of chocolate biscuits.

Kate's nose twitched and her eyes gleamed.

'I think I'd like a chocolate biscuit,' she said.

'I knew it!' grumbled Kamla, 'but leave some for me.'

When Kate's mother came to collect her she said to Kamla, 'Please thank your mother very much for having Kate, and I hope she didn't get up to any mischief.'

Kamla told her mother who smiled and said, 'Mischief! Mischief!' and laughed.

34

Just before they stepped outside, Kate sniffed the air.

'Your house doesn't smell so bad now,' she said. 'Goodbye. See you tomorrow.'

4

The Big Brown Trunk

Kamla had already been sent back to bed three times. But it was no good – she couldn't sleep, and when she couldn't sleep she found it impossible to stay in bed.

She lay on her tummy, peering down through the banisters, catching snatches of conversation and laughter.

What a day it had been! Her big cousin, Leela, had just arrived from India on a visit. The excitement had been tremendous.

Earlier in the day, the whole family had gone to the airport to meet her. Even some aunts and uncles from the North had turned up. They brought garlands of yellow flowers with them to drape round Leela's neck and welcome her in true Indian style!

When Leela walked out of the customs hall there was a gasp of delight. No one had seen her since she was a little girl like Kamla.

Now, here was a beautiful lady with a long, thick, black plait which fell to her waist, swishing through the doors in a glittering saree.

She was pushing a trolley with her luggage on it. There didn't seem to be very much – just one shoulder bag and one big, brown trunk with stickers all over it!

Kamla had suddenly felt shy and hung back behind her mother, as her beautiful cousin was garlanded and kissed. When Leela bent to kiss her, she was aware of a rich scent of flowers and perfume all mixed up. It made her think of India, even though she had never been there.

They had all piled into her father's car to go home. Leela's big, brown trunk was so big that Daddy couldn't shut the boot properly because it stuck out. Daddy had to tie the boot with string to keep it down!

Later, back at home, everyone had been very kind and polite to Leela. They made sure she had a nice cup of tea, and they sat her down in the most comfy chair. But really, they were all dying to know what was inside Leela's big, brown trunk!

At last Leela had dragged the trunk into

the middle of the room. She knelt on the carpet, turned the key in the lock and lifted the lid. It was as if she had opened a treasure chest! Everyone peered into it, bursting with curiosity.

Then she had lifted up shining sarees, embroidered tunics and shirts, brightly coloured ties and boxes of bangles. There was something for everyone. Soon the living room was strewn with delights like a dazzling bazaar!

Leela's trunk seemed bottomless. Still she delved. She pulled out a large box of Indian sweets, and, joy of joys, a whole bag of spices specially and lovingly ground by her grandmother. Leela handed the spices to Kamla's mother who couldn't have looked happier if she had been handed a bag of gold.

At last Leela had got up, holding a package. 'Where is Kamla?' she had called in her high, silvery voice. 'This is for you.'

Kamla had stepped forward, her hands tightly clasped. What had Leela brought for her?

She took the package and held it close for a moment. She always liked to try and guess what was inside a parcel before opening it.

But now everyone was shouting, 'Open it! Open it! Come on, Kamla, don't keep us all in suspense!'

So Kamla had quickly torn off the wrapping paper, and everyone had sighed with pleasure at what they saw. There lay a pair of shiny, satin, pink pyjamas with a tunic to match.

The tunic was embroidered all down the front with tiny white beads and silver sequins which sparkled like stars. There was a long, flimsy, paler pink veil, also dotted with sequins. This was for tossing over your shoulders, or draping round your head. It was the sort of costume little Indian girls wear until they are old enough to go into sarees.

Kamla couldn't believe there was anything in the world as pretty. She put the costume on immediately. It felt shiny and cold. She paraded round the living room while everyone admired her.

'Please can I go and show it to Kate?' she had begged.

But mother had said firmly, 'Show her tomorrow. It's way past your bedtime. Say goodnight!'

So Kamla had gone upstairs to bed. She had tried to sleep but couldn't.

Downstairs, everyone was eating a special rice and curry which her mother had prepared in Leela's honour. There was multi-coloured pulauo rice filled with nuts and raisins and delicate spices; there was rich meat curry made with jogurt and coconut, and all sorts of smaller silver dishes filled with vegetables and pickles and mouth-watering chutneys.

Lying there on the landing, Kamla secretly watched her mother whisking to and fro from the kitchen to the dining room. She caught glimpses of Leela as the door opened and shut. Once Leela saw her and winked, but didn't give her away!

Later, everyone went into the living room. They flopped on the carpet around Kamla's father who got out his accordian and began to play. Leela curled up next to him. She tucked her feet inside her saree and began to sing. Someone beat a rhythm on the lid of Leela's trunk, as if it were a drum.

As her sweet voice carried its strange melodies up the stairs, Kamla's eyes at last began to feel heavy. She crept back to her room and slipped into bed. She was asleep even before she had time to pull the covers over herself.

At school the next day, Kamla couldn't stop talking about her big cousin Leela and the marvels that came out of her big, brown trunk. She told her teacher, and she told the dinner ladies and of course she told Kate.

By the end of the day, Kate was dying to see cousin Leela, and this big, brown trunk which had brought such marvellous things!

'Come round and play after school,' suggested Kamla. 'Then you'll be able to see Leela.'

Leela met the girls at the door when they got home. She was pleased to meet Kate. Kamla had told her all about Kate over breakfast.

Kamla rushed upstairs. A few moments later she had torn off her grey cardigan, her grey pinafore dress and her school socks and shoes. She came slowly downstairs like a queen wearing her new shiny, pink satin pyjamas and tunic with the veil tossed loosely round her shoulders.

Kate goggled in amazement.

42

'Did that come out of the big, brown trunk?' she cried. Then she walked round and round her friend, fingering the delicate veil and smoothing her hand over the cool satin.

Then Kate whispered to Kamla that she wanted to see the big, brown trunk.

'It's upstairs,' hissed Kamla. 'Follow me.'

The two girls bounded upstairs and rushed into Leela's room. 'It's under the bed,' cried Kamla. So they flopped down on the floor on their tummies and peered under the counterpane.

'It's very big,' whispered Kate. 'Is it empty now?'

'I'm not sure,' replied Kamla.

'What are you two up to?' exclaimed Leela, coming in.

'I was showing Kate your big, brown trunk,' cried Kamla jumping up. 'I told her how it was full of wonderful things, like a treasure chest! I told her that my tunic and pyjamas had come out of it. Have you got any pyjamas for Kate?'

Leela got down on her knees and pulled the trunk out from under the bed.

43

'Are you going to open it?' asked Kate excitedly.

'This treasure chest, as you call it, may have something in it for you, though not pyjamas, I'm afraid,' murmured Leela.

Kate watched, hardly daring to breathe, as the catches flew open and Leela lifted the lid. She rummaged round for a few moments among her sarees and blouses, and then said, 'Ah! This is what I was looking for!'

She got up holding a shining, white veil shot with silver threads which sparkled in the sunlight.

'Can I keep it?' squeaked Kate. She could hardly believe her eyes.

'Yes,' said Leela, smiling. 'Because you're Kamla's best friend.'

Kamla helped Kate toss the glittering veil round her shoulders.

'All you need now are the tunic and pyjamas, and then you'd really look Indian!'

'I've got pyjamas! I'll go and put them on!' and Kate dashed off home leaving Kamla and Leela looking puzzled.

After a while she was back. Kamla and Leela clapped their hands with delight.

There stood Kate in her own pink flannel-
ette pyjamas! She didn't seem to mind that
the pyjama top had little blue engines chug-
ging all over it! Across her shoulders she had
tossed the beautiful white and silver veil which
Leela had given her.

'There you are!' cried Kate proudly. 'Now
I look Indian!'

'You look lovely!' exclaimed Leela.

'Thank you very much for the veil,' said

Kate. 'It's the most beautiful thing I've ever had.'

'I told you that Leela's big, brown trunk was a treasure chest,' laughed Kamla.

'Let's go downstairs now,' said Leela, pushing the big, brown trunk back under the bed. 'I've been making all sorts of nice goodies for tea.'

5
The Tooth Trick

'I've got a wobbly tooth,' said Kate, and she opened her mouth and wobbled a bottom, front tooth with her finger.

Kamla tried wobbling her teeth, but not one would wobble.

'When my tooth comes out, I'll put it under my pillow and then a fairy will come in the night and leave me ten pence,' said Kate proudly.

Kamla prodded even harder at one of her teeth. She wanted a fairy to come and leave her ten pence too, but it was no use. Not one of her teeth would budge even a little.

Kate wobbled her tooth all day. Whenever Kamla looked at her, she could see Kate's pink tongue pushing the loose tooth backwards and forwards, backwards and forwards.

She wobbled it in class while she did her writing; she wobbled it in the playground in front of all her friends, and she wobbled it all the way home from school.

Kate went to play at Kamla's house after school that day. When they got home, they rushed straight upstairs to Kamla's bedroom.

'Let's make a house today!' said Kamla.

'Yes, let's!' agreed Kate.

There was a table in Kamla's room on which she did her drawing, painting, jigsaws and plasticine. But Kamla liked playing under her table as much as playing on top of it.

She dragged the coverlet off her bed and draped it over the table, and that made two walls, front and back; then she dragged a blanket off her bed and draped it the other way across, making up four walls altogether.

Then the two girls crept inside and felt all cosy in their dark, little house.

'We need to make two beds,' said Kate.

'I'll fetch some pillows,' said Kamla. She crawled out and got two pillows. The two girls lay down side by side with their heads on the pillows.

'Goodnight, Kamla.'

'Goodnight, Kate.'

Then Kamla sat up and nearly bumped her head.

'I feel like a cup of tea. I'll go and get my tea-set. She crawled out of the little house and ran to her toy cupboard.

The tea-set was kept carefully in its box on an upper shelf because it was made of real china, and had a blue willow pattern design on the four little cups, the four little saucers, the four little plates, the tea-pot, the milk jug and the sugar bowl.

Kamla filled the tea-pot and milk jug with

water from the bathroom tap, then she crawled very carefully back into the house on her knees and elbows, trying not to spill any.

Kate was still lying on her pillow wobbling her tooth with her tongue.

'I think my tooth is going to come out soon,' she said, and gave Kamla a big grin so that Kamla could see her tooth hanging all lop-sided over her bottom lip.

Kamla's mother came upstairs to tell the girls tea was ready.

'But we're having tea already in our little house,' wailed Kamla. 'Please can we have something up here?'

So Kamla's mother brought them up some bread and butter and a chocolate biscuit each to eat in their own little house off their own little plates, but she said firmly if they wanted more than just water to drink from the toy tea-pot, then they must come downstairs.

Kamla and Kate sat happily in their little house munching their sandwiches when suddenly Kate shrieked, 'Ow!'

She had just taken a bite on her wobbly tooth. Her tongue immediately went in search of the tooth, but all it found was a gummy gap. The tooth had gone!

'My tooth! It's gone!' screamed Kate. 'Oh where is it? If I can't find it, I won't be able to

put it under my pillow tonight, and I won't get ten pence from the fairies!'

She crawled round and round in circles in the squashed little space under the table, bumping her head, knocking over the tea-pot with her bottom and kneeling in the bread and butter, making her knees all buttery.

'Where's my tooth?' she wailed.

'Oh, stop it, Kate!' cried Kamla crossly, trying to rescue her precious cups and saucers. 'Look out! You're going to break my tea-set! Look at the mess you're making!'

'But I must find my tooth,' wailed Kate.

Kamla's mother heard the commotion all the way downstairs and came up to see what was happening.

'What is the matter?' she asked, running anxiously into the room.

Kamla explained all about Kate's tooth. Then her mother understood. She pulled the coverlet and blanket off the house, bent down and picked up the four little cups, saucers, and plates, and the tea-pot, milk jug and sugar bowl, and tried to scrape the squashed bread and butter from the carpet.

Suddenly she cried out, 'Here! Tooth!' pointing to the squashed sandwich. Carefully she pulled out a tiny, little, white tooth which was embedded in the bread and butter.

'My tooth! You've found it! Oh thank you,' cried Kate. 'Now I really will get ten pence from the fairies.' And she popped the tooth safely into her pocket.

Kamla looked cross, and tried once more to wobble her tooth, but it was no use.

While Kate went to the bathroom to rinse her mouth, Kamla's mother helped tidy Kamla's bedroom and put away the tea-set. Then they went downstairs to have a proper tea.

The next day at school Kate was all bubbly and excited.

'The fairies came in the night,' she told Kamla and her friends. 'They took my tooth, and look what they left!' She held up a new, shiny ten pence piece.

'You are lucky,' moaned Kamla. 'None of my teeth is even loose. I won't get ten pence for ages. Why do the fairies want baby teeth anyway?'

'I don't know,' said Kate. 'Perhaps they collect lots of teeth together and make a necklace. My Mum has a necklace made of sharks' teeth.'

Over the next few weeks another of Kate's teeth became wobbly, and then another. Some other children in the class were beginning to lose teeth too.

Kate began to look very comical. Everytime she laughed, she showed a great big gap, and it made her speak funnily. She was also becoming quite rich.

'I've got forty pence now from the tooth fairies,' she told Kamla.

Kamla went home and grumbled to her mother. 'It's not fair,' she moaned, 'Kate has lost four teeth and she's getting lots of money from the tooth fairies. When are my teeth going to fall out?'

'I don't know, darling,' said her mother. 'Be patient. You will lose your first teeth in the end, everybody does, and then you'll be as rich as Kate.'

When Kate lost another tooth, that was too much, Kamla almost burst into tears.

'I've got an idea,' said Kate, trying to comfort her friend. 'Why don't you pretend to lose a tooth. Find a little button or a stone and put it under your pillow. Perhaps the fairies won't notice in the dark, and they'll leave you ten pence anyway.'

Kamla's eyes shone. 'What a good idea! Come and help me find something.'

They looked through both their mothers' work baskets, but although there were lots

55

of buttons, they were either too big, or too round, or the wrong colour, or just too much like a button.

'The fairies won't be fooled by those. They're not stupid, are they!' said Kamla mournfully.

'Let's look in the garden, then,' suggested Kate.

They went to Kate's garden and then to Kamla's garden. But although they spent ages sifting through the soil till their fingernails were black, somehow they just could not find a stone that looked anything like a tooth.

Kate frowned. 'I saw lots of white stones once, now where was it!' She thought and thought and then finally gave a shout. 'I know! It was at the sea-side. And not just stones but shells! I made a collection and brought it home. Come and look.'

The two girls raced up to Kate's bedroom. She rushed to her shelf and took down a pretty, green box. They both peered inside.

It was full of pebbles and shells of every shape and form. There were long, purply ones, round ridged ones like saucers, big, curly whirly ones in which you could hear the sea if you put them to your ear, and suddenly, there at the bottom, some tiny white bits of shell like fragments of pearl.

Kate sifted them gently with a finger until Kamla shouted, 'That one! That looks just like a tooth!'

Kate examined the shell lying on Kamla's hand. 'Yes, that looks just like a tooth. I'm sure the fairies won't know the difference. Put it under your pillow tonight and see what happens.'

That night Kamla slipped the shell under

her pillow as Kate had told her. Then she lay awake as long as she could, hoping and wishing that the tooth fairy would come, but soon she was fast asleep.

The next morning Kamla woke early. At first she lay quietly listening to the birds. Then she remembered! She leapt up and flung her pillow aside. Had the tooth fairy been? The shell had gone, but there was no shiny ten pence piece in its place.

Kamla burst into tears.

'I suppose the tooth fairies are used to tricks,' said her mother comfortingly when she heard Kamla wailing.

Kamla walked glumly to school that morning and met Kate on the way. Kate rushed up with her gappy, toothless grin.

'Did it work?' she cried. 'Did you get ten pence?'

'No,' grunted Kamla sulkily. 'It didn't work, though they took the shell!' And she walked on with her head and her eyes down.

Suddenly, she stopped. There was something glinting in the gutter. She ran forwards to have a look. It was a silver five pence piece, just lying there!

'Look what I've found!' shrieked Kamla with excitement.

'It must be from the fairies,' cried Kate. 'They wanted to show you that they didn't fall for your trick, but they've given you five pence for the shell!'

Kamla's mother nodded and smiled encouragingly.

'You see Kamla! You haven't been forgotten. Your time will come.'

A few days later, Kamla bounced into school beaming all over her face!

'You're looking pleased,' remarked Kate curiously. 'Did you find another five pence?'

'No!' laughed Kamla, opening her mouth and putting in a finger, 'but I've got a wobbly tooth!'

6

A Look at the Moon

It was a beautiful, bright, clear night. Not very late – but because it was winter, the moon and stars were already up long before Kamla and Kate were ready for bed.

Kamla had been playing at Kate's house when her father came to fetch her home. Kate's father came out to greet him, and the two of them stood at the gate looking up at the glittering sky.

'I wish I knew the names of all those stars,' sighed Kamla's father.

'On a clear night like this it's easy to recognise them,' replied Kate's dad. 'That big, low star over there is Venus– the evening star; those two there, one above the other, are the twins, Castor and Pollux! There's the Plough! Trying to work out a group of stars like the Plough is like trying to draw a line dot to dot in Kamla's activity book! Over there – three across and two down – is Orion's Belt, and that very faint far cluster of stars is the Seven Sisters.'

'You do know a lot,' breathed Mr. Gupta admiringly. 'In India, the stars and planets are very important to us. We think they influence our lives and futures. We always know our horoscope, and yet I've never learned to recognise the stars in the sky!'

'I have a telescope, you know,' said Kate's father. 'Would you like to look through it?'

'I would indeed!' exclaimed Mr. Gupta.

'You girls go on playing for a little longer,' said Mr. Caldicott, 'while I take Kamla's father upstairs to show him my telescope.'

'I love looking through my Dad's telescope,' said Kate. 'I like looking at the moon. You can see all the mountains and the craters clear as anything.'

'I wish I could have a look,' murmured Kamla, wonderingly. 'Have you seen any spacemen up there?'

'No!' laughed Kate, 'though I always hope I'll see something moving. The moon looks so still and lonely. My Dad says it has mountains and valleys just like we do, and yet there are no trees, no grass, no birds or animals – nothing alive at all!'

The two girls looked up into the night sky at the full, round moon.

'I can see some mountains!' cried Kamla excitedly. 'I wish I could go there!'

'My Dad says we might, one day,' said Kate thoughtfully. 'He says we might be able to go on holiday to the moon. They might do package tours! One day.'

'Perhaps they have good beaches, and seas for swimming!' chattered Kamla, who loved swimming more than anything!

'I don't think there's any water up there,' said Kate. 'There isn't even any air.'

'Well how can you go on holiday there then?' moaned Kamla.

'We'd have to wear space suits and take our own air! Like taking a packed lunch!' laughed Kate.

The two fathers came downstairs again. 'Come on Kamla!' cried Mr. Gupta. 'We must be off. Goodbye Mr. Caldicott, thank you for showing me the telescope.'

'You must come and look through it again,' said Kate's father warmly. 'There is an eclipse of the moon next month – that should be interesting.'

'Can I look through your telescope please, Mr. Caldicott?' asked Kamla.

'Of course you can, Kamla – another day when you have more time.'

Kate and her father stayed at the garden gate for a while, looking up at the sky.

'Funny to think that when I was a kid like you, men hadn't got to the moon,' said Dad, 'and I used to think there were moon people and men from Mars! Even scientists used to think there may be vegetable life on Mars – walking cabbages!'

'How awful!' shrieked Kate.

'Not really,' laughed Dad. 'Why should we think all life looks like us?'

'If I saw a walking cabbage I'd die of fright!' shuddered Kate.

'What I'd really like to see is a space ship coming from another planet,' sighed her father. 'When you look up at the sky and see all those millions of stars, it's hard to believe that only our little planet has life on it. I hope there is more life somewhere out there, even if it is just a cabbage!'

They walked back thoughtfully into the kitchen. Dad opened the oven and got out a shepherd's pie for the two of them. Mum was at evening classes and would be late back, so Kate and Dad sat down together still thinking about space.

Dad was just about to put a spoonful of cabbage on her plate when Kate cried out, 'No, Dad, no! That cabbage might be clever!'

'Don't be daft, Kate!' smiled Dad, putting it on anyway. 'If you don't eat it, you won't be clever. Now, come on! It's only a spoonful!'

'Dad, how would you know if a space ship was coming from another planet?' asked Kate.

'I suppose you'd see the lights winking and moving,' said Dad. 'You never see the stars move, except of course a shooting star!'

After supper Kate went upstairs to get ready for bed. She stood at her bedroom window looking up at the moon and stars. If only she could see the winking lights of a space ship. But what if the space ship was being flown by cabbages? What then? 'Could I really make friends with a cabbage?' thought Kate to herself.

Suddenly she heard clicking heels on the pavement below. Mum was back. Kate dashed into bed and lay there, pretending to be asleep. Mum was rather a long time downstairs before she finally came up to peep at Kate, by which time Kate was nearly asleep.

As her mother tucked her in and kissed her head, Kate murmured, 'What do cabbages think about?'

Before her startled mother could think of anything to say, Kate was fast asleep.

'Can I see through the telescope today?' Kamla asked Kate as they walked home from school.

'You can when Dad comes home,' replied Kate. 'I'm not allowed into his telescope room unless he's there.'

After tea, Kamla called round at Kate's house. 'Is your Dad back yet?'

'No, not yet, but do stay and play with me,' begged Kate.

So the two friends played 'house', then they dressed up, and then they pretended they were on the moon. But all the time Kamla only wanted to look through the telescope.

It began to get dark. Kamla stopped playing and stood in the window gazing up at the moon.

'Are you sure your Dad will mind if we have just a little peep through the telescope?' she pleaded. 'It will soon be time for me to go home.'

'Oh, all right,' Kate said, giving in. 'Just one quick peep and don't tell anyone or there'll be trouble!'

The two girls checked first that Kate's

mother would not notice. No, she was busy making supper. They tiptoed upstairs.

'I don't remember seeing a room with a telescope,' said Kamla, who thought she knew Kate's house from top to bottom.

'Dad made a special room in the roof last summer,' whispered Kate. 'Look!'

Kamla looked up to see a trap door and a ladder slung across the ceiling. Kate reached up on tiptoe and just managed to unfold the ladder down to the ground.

'What do we do now?' asked Kamla nervously.

'We climb the ladder,' announced Kate. 'Come on!'

'Perhaps we'd better wait for your Dad after all,' quavered Kamla.

'Oh, come on! It's easy! I've done it tons of times,' urged Kate, and she began to climb. When she had climbed about four steps she pushed aside the trap door, and clambered into the roof. Looking up from below, Kamla could see the telescope. It stood like a large, long-legged insect on a tripod, its long, black body pointing upwards through a skylight window to the vast, black universe above.

Kamla scrambled up the ladder. Kate already had her eye to the telescope.

'Let me have a go!' begged Kamla, jumping up next to her. Kate moved over and Kamla stuck her face up to the viewfinder.

'I can't see a thing,' she grumbled.

'You have to shut one eye, and look through the other,' advised Kate.

Kamla tried to shut one eye but only screwed up her face instead. 'This is hopeless, I can't do it!' she wailed.

'Cover one eye with your hand,' suggested Kate.

Kamla did. She tried looking again. 'I . . . think . . . I can see . . . something,' she said warily. 'It's a little bit blurry.'

'If I twist this bit of the telescope it should make it clearer,' said Kate.

'That's it! It's coming . . . it's a star . . . a big, yellow star . . . oh no! It's not a star, it's the lampost,' growled Kamla.

'You must have moved it,' said Kate. 'Tip it up a bit.'

Kamla tried again. 'Ah! Now I'm looking at the moon . . . I think. Can you get it clearer?'

Kate twisted again. 'Can you see the mountains and craters?' she asked.

'Yes, yes I can! I can see the valleys too – and the deserts – it's wonderful!

'Let me have a look now,' cried Kate.

'Wait a minute, I've seen something else. The telescope began to wobble about as Kate pointed it this way and that. 'Whoops I've lost it . . . no, got it!'

'Hurry up and let me see,' hissed Kate impatiently. 'Dad will be back soon.'

Suddenly Kamla shrieked. 'I've got it – it's a moving light. It must be a space ship!'

'Let me see,' said Kate pushing Kamla aside. 'Where? I can't see anything!'

Kamla began to twist the focus. 'Can't you see it?'

'Wait! Yes, I can. I've got the moving light!'

'It must be a space ship mustn't it?' insisted Kamla.

'It can't be a shooting star – they go as quick as a flash,' murmured Kate. 'And proper stars don't move around the sky, so it must be a space ship. Oh, I wish Dad was here. He said he'd like to see one more than anything else,' cried Kate, jumping up and down. 'The cabbages are coming! Hooray!'

'SSh!' hissed Kamla as she heard the front door. 'Your Dad's back!' But it was too late. Mr. Caldicott was already leaping up the stairs to see what was going on.

'What are you two doing up there?' he called angrily.

'Oh, Dad, quick!' yelled Kate. 'Come and look through the telescope, I've seen a moving light. It must be a space ship!'

Kate's father heaved himself up the ladder. Kamla and Kate stood aside as he put his eye to the telescope. They waited, breathlessly, wonderingly. Is it? Could it be? He pointed one way, then fiddled and pointed another. He scanned the whole horizon with the telescope. Suddenly he stopped and twisted the focus.

'Aah!' he gave a long sigh. 'Aah! I see!'

'Is it a space ship?' squealed Kamla.

'With walking cabbages?' added Kate.

Mr. Caldicott took his eye away from the telescope and looked down at the two excited faces.

'No, my dears, I'm sorry to disappoint you.

71

It's not a space ship, or a flying saucer or any other kind of unidentified flying object, with or without cabbages, it's a straightforward aeroplane!'

'Oh!' Kate's face fell a mile.

'All aeroplanes have lights at night, just like cars. You saw an aeroplane moving through the sky.'

Kate looked up at her father wondering if he was now going to be angry and tell them off, but instead he smiled and patted her head.

'I'll tell you one thing though, it's every star-gazer's dream to be the one to see the first space ship from another planet. I'll let you come again and look if you promise to wait until I'm there too.'

'I wish I had a telescope in my roof,' said Kamla wistfully, 'I'd like to be a star gazer.'

'Then you'd better learn to shut one eye,' retorted Kate as they all climbed back down the ladder.

'I wonder if somewhere out there in space on one of those stars there's a cabbage having trouble closing one eye as he looks at us through his telescope,' laughed Kamla.

'I don't know about cabbages, but I do know there's a lovely smell coming from the kitchen, and it's not cabbage!' cried Mr. Caldicott. 'Let's go down and see what it is. I'm starving!'

7
Kamla and Kate Dress Up

Clip clop! Clip clop! 'What's that noise coming down the road?' thought Kamla. It sounded a bit like a pony, but not quite. She ran to the gate to see.

Clip clop! Clip clop! It was Kate, clip-clopping down the road in her mother's high heel shoes.

'I've been dressing-up!' called Kate.

'I can see that!' cried Kamla, looking at her friend. She was wearing a skirt that dragged on the ground and blouse that was miles too big for her, and on her head was her mother's best straw hat.

Kate tottered up to Kamla. 'Why don't you dress up too?' she asked, clutching the skirt which had begun to slip.

'My Mum doesn't wear skirts and blouses like that,' said Kamla, 'but I suppose I could wear one of her sarees.'

Kamla ran upstairs to her mother's bedroom with Kate pulling herself up the banister behind her, trying not to trip over her skirt.

Kamla opened the wardrobe. It was full of beautiful sarees all neatly folded on hangers.

'Wear that one – it's beautiful!' cried Kate pointing to a scarlet and gold saree.

'I'd better not,' sighed Kamla. 'That's my mother's wedding saree.'

'That's a nice one!' said Kate and pulled out a silky blue and turquoise saree. It tumbled to the floor in a glistening heap. 'How do you put it on?'

Kamla picked up one end. 'You sort of tuck it in and wrap it round and make some pleats and tuck them in and toss the rest over your shoulder ...' she muttered as she struggled like a trapped insect among the slippery folds.

After a while she had managed to get most of the saree tucked into her belt and wrapped round her. It made her look fatter than usual but then she had so much to tuck in. But when the last yard was draped loosely round her shoulders and over her head it didn't show too much.

'How do I look?' asked Kamla.

'You look like a princess!' sighed Kate. 'I wish my Mum wore sarees.'

'Let's go out!' said Kamla boldly.

'I don't dare!' giggled Kate. 'People might laugh.'

'No, they won't – you look lovely. Come on, let's go to the swings!'

So Kate straightened her hat and gave an extra yank to her skirt so as not to trip over it, and Kamla gave one last tuck at the wodge of

saree pressing into her tummy then she slipped on some flip flops and off they went.

Clip clop! Clip clop! went Kate's high heels down the road.

F-lip f-lop! F-lip f-lop! went Kamla's flip flops alongside her.

They passed Miss Gilpin's house on the corner. The old lady was sitting in the window as usual and waved to them. They went into her garden and bobbed in front of her so that she could see their dressing-up clothes.

Miss Gilpin nodded and smiled, 'You do look nice!' she called through the window.

Then they carried on to the park. As they drew nearer they could hear music.

'That sounds like a brass band,' said Kate.

'Or a steel band,' said Kamla.

It turned out to be both. 'What's going on?' asked the girls as they hurried closer.

The park was crowded with people. Then Kamla and Kate realised that most of them were dressed up! There were cubs and brownies and nurses and farmers, and soldiers and spacemen, and people wearing costumes from other countries, all milling around excitedly.

Out in the road was a line of lorries

decorated so magnificently that you could hardly tell they were lorries. The front lorry had a huge banner slung across with the word, CARNIVAL. Then, suddenly, a commanding voice rang out through a loud hailer.

'Our Carnival procession is about to begin. Will everyone please take their positions on the floats as soon as possible.'

There was a flurry of activity as people scattered in all directions to get to their various floats. Kamla and Kate found themselves swept along in the crowd.

Suddenly Kate noticed a float which was more magnificent than any of the others. It was decorated in silver and gold like a fairy-tale castle; it had walls and turrets with little flags fluttering in the wind. Sitting on a high throne in the middle was a big girl who was in the top class at their school. She was dressed as a queen in a long satin dress. She had a scarlet cloak over her shoulders and a gold crown on her head.

'Look, Kamla! That's Sharon from our school! Doesn't she look lovely!' cried Kate. They ran towards her, calling her name. 'Hello Sharon!'

At that moment a voice said, 'You must be the ladies-in-waiting for the May Queen. We must get you into place quickly, it's time to go.' And before anyone could say a word, Kamla and Kate found themselves heaved up on to the gold and silver float.

Sharon looked in amazement at the two friends. 'What on earth are you doing here?' she said.

'I don't know,' said Kate looking mystified.

'We only came to look!' exclaimed Kamla.

Sharon tried to call someone to help Kamla and Kate get down again, but her voice was drowned by the loud hailer ordering everyone to stand by!

The band struck up a loud march, and the float began to move.

'Oh dear!' cried Sharon. 'It's too late to do anything now, you'll just have to be in the procession.'

'Crumbs!' muttered Kate.

'What will our mothers say?' quavered Kamla.

'Come on,' cried Sharon. 'It's no good standing there all in a muddle. You might as well be my handmaidens now that you're

79

here. Stand one on each side of my throne and wave.'

Kamla and Kate did as they were told. As the lorry turned out of the park gates into the road it gave a slight jerk making Kate's hat slip over her eyes.

'Whoops!' she said, pushing it back into place, and Kamla who had nearly felt like crying, began to laugh.

The line of floats snaked its way out into the main road and headed for the High Street. Crowds and crowds of people had gathered, and soon the air was filled with cheering and shouting and whistles of admiration.

'Come on, wave you two!' cried the May Queen, who was waving with a white gloved hand as if she'd been born to it.

Kamla and Kate began to wave too, feeling glamorous and excited.

Kate's mother was out doing the weekend shopping. She thought her daughter was at Kamla's house quietly dressing-up. As the parade went by she stopped to look, and had the shock of her life.

'Good Heavens!' she shrieked. 'There's Kate!'

The lorry went slowly by with Kate waving and smiling, all dressed up in her mother's clothes and the best straw hat she'd bought for a wedding!

'Kate!' screamed her mother, 'what on earth are you doing up there?'

But Kate didn't hear her above the din of the brass band in front and the steel band behind, and she didn't see her among all the other hundreds of faces gazing up at the procession.

Kamla's father was returning home from his shift at the factory. He, too, paused to watch the procession.

'Don't I recognise that greeny blue saree up there?' he thought, as he watched the float passing by. 'I most certainly do! Kamla!' he bellowed. 'What are you doing on the back of a lorry and in one of your mother's best sarees?'

But Kamla was too busy smiling and waving to notice her angry father leaping up and down in the crowd.

The carnival procession finished in front of

the Town Hall. The Lord Mayor and Lady Mayoress were waiting in their gold chains to greet them.

Photographers crowded forward with light bulbs flashing as they took pictures for their newspapers.

Kamla and Kate were lifted down from the lorry.

'My saree's coming apart!' squealed Kamla, desperately tucking in all round.

'I've lost a shoe!' yelled Kate, who was walking all unevenly – one up, one down.

Click! Click! A camera was pointing at them.

'Buy the Gazette next Thursday and you'll see yourselves,' beamed a photographer.

At that moment Kate's mother, and Kamla's father appeared.

Kamla and Kate clutched each other's hand.

'M-mummy looks m-mad!' stammered Kate.

'So does my Dad!' groaned Kamla.

Suddenly the Lady Mayoress swooped down, her gold chain swinging merrily.

'My dears!' she cried, putting an arm

round each girl. 'You were both wonderful! You must be proud of them,' she beamed at their parents.

'Well – yes!' said Kate's mother.

'Actually – yes!' agreed Kamla's dad, straightening his tie.

'We were only dressing-up,' said Kate.

'We didn't mean to go far,' said Kamla.

'Ice-creams all round!' announced the Mayor.

They found themselves swept into the Town Hall for ice-cream and orange squash.

'Next time we should dress up as trapeze artists and circus pony riders, then we might land up in a circus,' whispered Kate.

'That would be good,' breathed Kamla.

'Oh, no, you don't!' laughed Kate's Mum. 'No more wandering off like that or you'll be sorry!'

8

The Boy Who Walked On His Hands

One Monday morning Kamla and Kate skipped into their classroom. They each held a sprig of new, sticky, spring buds for Mrs. Stevens.

Suddenly Kate said, 'Look! Is that a new boy?'

Standing by their teacher's desk was a dark boy in long, grey trousers and a checked shirt. But there was something a little strange about him to Kate.

'Look at his hair!' she said.

The boy's long, black hair was wound tightly round into a top knot and tied up with a neat handkerchief.

'He must be a Sikh boy,' said Kamla knowingly. 'Sikh boys must never cut their hair. Their religion says so.'

'Will it grow and grow right down to his toes?' asked Kate in amazement.

'I suppose so,' replied Kamla. 'I've never seen a man with his hair loose. It's always tied up in a turban or a knot. My Dad's best friend at work wears a turban. He's a Sikh. He's called Mr. Singh.'

Mrs. Stevens saw Kamla and called her over. 'Kamla! You're just the person I was looking for. I want you to be a great help to me and look after this new boy who is joining our class. His name is Amrik Singh. He

arrived from India three days ago and he speaks no English. I hope you can understand him and be my translator.'

'His name is "Singh" too, like your Dad's friend. Is he a relation?' asked Kate.

'My father says, "All Sikhs are Singhs, but all Singhs aren't Sikhs!"' said Kamla, 'so he probably isn't a relation.'

She went over to the new boy, holding Kate's hand because she suddenly felt shy. Then she saw Amrik's eyes fill with tears and she immediately spoke to him in Hindi.

'Hello Amrik. My name's Kamla. This is my best friend, Kate. Don't worry. I'll look after you.'

Then Mrs. Stevens spoke to the whole class. 'Children! I want you to meet a new boy. His name is Amrik Singh and he has only just arrived from India. Everything here is very strange to him, and he speaks no English. But we are very lucky because Kamla not only speaks English as well as you do, she also speaks Hindi. Amrik can understand Hindi, so Kamla will be our interpreter. But I want you all to help Amrik to learn English as quickly as possible.'

Kamla and Kate took Amrik over to their table. He sat down rather awkwardly. At his village school in India all the children used to sit cross-legged on the ground under the mango tree.

Kamla pointed to each child on her table and introduced them.

'This is Kate, Justin, Nigel and Rachel,' she said. Then she prodded the table and said, 'and this is our table!'

Amrik looked solemnly at each child. 'Kate, Jus ... teen, Ni ... gel, Rachel ...' then he prodded the table and said, 'Our table!' Everyone laughed and clapped.

At playtime Kamla and Kate took Amrik out into the playground. He stood in a corner with his back to the wall looking very frightened. Ever since he arrived in England he had felt puzzled. He could see no brown earth under his feet – just concrete. Wherever you walked, the ground was hard. No wonder his father had made him wear shoes and socks. He could hardly see the sky. It seemed lost up there between tall blocks of buildings, and the sky was the colour of the concrete – grey! In India you did not have to look for the earth and sky, it was all around you. And you could not lose the sun as they seemed to here.

'Kamla, where is the earth? Where are the wheatfields? Where do they grow rice and mustard seed? Where are the fruit trees? The mango and guava groves? Can oxen plough this hard ground? How do you eat?'

'We live in a city, Amrik,' explained Kamla. 'The food is grown in the countryside. We buy our wheat and rice and fruit from the shops.'

'Where are the water wells?' asked Amrik looking around. 'I'm thirsty. Are the wells also under all this hard stone?' He looked in despair around the playground.

'We've got a water fountain. Come on! I'll show you.'

Kamla dragged him round a corner where a cluster of children were taking it in turns to drink from the fountain. Amrik watched in astonishment as one by one the children pressed a mysterious knob and from out of a concrete, round pedestal a silver jet of water arched into their open mouths.

'Hasn't he even seen a water fountain before?' asked Kate.

'No,' said Kamla. 'He comes from a village where all the water is pulled out of a well in buckets.'

'Goodness!' murmured Kate. 'It must be like coming to another planet!'

So the morning passed. Kamla was very good at being an interpreter, and Kate enjoyed being a teacher and helping Amrik to say English words. By lunch time he could say, 'What is your name? My name is Amrik. How old are you? I am seven.' And of course, he learnt the word, water.

The lunch bell rang, and the children joined a queue, hopping up and down with hunger. Smells wafted out from the kitchen making their tummies rumble, but Amrik didn't understand these smells. They certainly weren't cooking dahl and chapattis!

'It's lunch time, Amrik!' cried Kate, pointing to her mouth and patting her tummy. Amrik nodded and repeated, 'lunch time!' but he didn't look too happy about it.

Kamla brought a packed lunch, so she had to join a separate queue.

'Kate will look after you,' she explained.

The line of children shuffled closer to a serving table. Eager hands grabbed a plate from a large pile. Amrik watched as each child held out his plate while three dinner ladies in white aprons and caps each dolloped a spoonful of something on to it.

The first dolloped something white like a ball of cotton wool; the next dolloped something brown and juicy; and the third dolloped something green and watery. All Amrik could do was copy.

He took a plate and held it out.

Amrik then followed Kate and the others to a table. They were already holding two silver objects – one in each hand – and shovelling their food down as fast as they could. In two minutes the white stuff, the brown stuff and the green stuff had gone.

'What's for pudding?' yelled Kate.

'Jam tarts!' shouted Nigel.

'Goody!' roared everyone.

Then suddenly they noticed that Amrik was still sitting there looking at his plate. He hadn't eaten a thing! He hadn't even picked up his knife and fork!

'Hurry up, Amrik!' begged Kate. 'Eat! Eat!

We can't go out to play until everyone on our table has finished.'

Amrik looked up at her miserably. 'Our table,' he repeated. He lifted his right hand and dipped it into the potato. He tried to roll it in his fingers as he would have done if it were rice. But somehow it wouldn't roll, and he held his hand up in disgust as potato and gravy dripped from his fingers.

Quickly Amrik licked his fingers and looked round him. How were the others eating? Awkwardly he picked up the strange tools on each side of his plate.

'Look, Amrik!' whispered Kate. 'Like this!' And she showed him how to use a knife and fork.

Just then, Mrs. Stevens and Kamla came hurrying over.

'I'm afraid the meat today is beef, and Amrik's religion does not allow him to eat beef,' said Mrs. Stevens. 'Please tell him only to eat the potato and cabbage.'

Kamla sat down next to Amrik and began to explain.

'Poor Amrik,' sighed Kate. 'Will he have enough to eat?'

'I've got a spare chappati in my lunch box,' said Kamla. She opened her box and offered it to Amrik. For the first time that day, a broad smile broke across his face.

Out in the playground the children were enjoying their playtime. Some were kicking a ball, others were skipping and chanting 'salt, mustard, vinegar, pepper'. Sometimes Kamla and Kate played tag or hopscotch, but at the moment they mostly wanted to practise hand-stands up against the wall.

Amrik was too shy to join in anything. He stood in a corner just watching and watching. It was strange to think that only a week ago he had been running and chasing with his friends along the two mile dusty path through the fields which ran from his school to home.

Once home, his mother would have given him a chapatti and some dahl – lentils – and then he would have gone to work in the fields, helping dig the soil, or taking charge of the bullocks.

There was hardly any job that he hadn't already tried. He could drive the bullocks and the plough, he could draw water from the well, he could sow the wheat seed and in the evening he gathered fuel for the fire and even milked the buffalo.

Amrik watched Kamla and Kate practising their handstands. Up against the wall they went, giggling at each other as they went red in the face from being upside down!

Suddenly, Amrik leapt from his corner and went up on to his hands with his shirt hanging out, and his legs waving in the air.

'Look at Amrik!' someone shrieked. As everyone turned to look, Amrik began to walk round the playground on his hands!

How the children laughed and clapped. 'He's like a clown!' shouted one.

'How do you do it!' cried another.

'Watch me!' yelled Kate, doing a hand-stand away from the wall, and managed to walk several steps before toppling right over in a heap! Soon everybody seemed to be up-side down in the playground, and Amrik had to walk round on his hands again and again.

The teachers peeped out of their staff room window, wondering what all the hullabaloo was about; the dinner ladies stopped their washing-up to have a look, and even the Headmistress let her coffee go cold because

she was so busy watching the new boy, Amrik Singh!

By the time playtime was over, Amrik had learned another sentence in English. It was, 'walk on your hands' because so many children had rushed up to him shouting over and over again, 'Amrik! Walk on your hands!'

Nigel looked admiringly at Amrik. More than anything he wanted to be friends with a boy who could walk on his hands.

'Can I sit next to Amrik?' Nigel asked Kate when they went in for afternoon lessons.

'All right,' said Kate shifting down one.

'Walk on your hands,' said Amrik to Nigel with a smile.

'No, Amrik, *you* walk on your hands,' laughed Nigel. 'I'll teach you to play football.'

9
Kamla's Secret

'What are you doing?' asked Kate.

'Oh, nothing,' said Kamla.

'You *were* doing something,' frowned Kate. 'You were twisting your hands in a funny way.'

'That's nothing,' repeated Kamla mysteriously. 'Come on! Let's play!'

The next day at school, while standing in the dinner line, Kate again noticed Kamla twisting her hands and arms. She had a far-away look on her face.

'You're doing it again,' cried Kate.

'Doing what?' asked Kamla.

'Doing this!' And Kate tried to twist her hands and arms as she had seen her friend doing.

Kamla laughed. 'Are you trying to be a snake?'

'No! I'm trying to copy you,' groaned Kate.

Then the line moved on and the dinner ladies served them their meat pie and mashed potatoes and they sat down to eat.

Afterwards, in the playground, Kate said crossly, 'I won't be your friend if you don't tell me what you were doing.'

'I was only trying to think how I could balance a stone on the palm of my hand, and twist my hand round in circles without letting the stone drop off,' explained Kamla.

'That's easy!' cried Kate. She picked up a small stone and tried. But as soon as her palm was twisted halfway round, pointing inwards, the stone fell off.

She tried again and again, but still the stone fell off.

'It's impossible!' she said.

Then Kamla had a go. She put the stone on the flat of her hand and held it outwards. Then slowly she began to twist her palm round in a circle. As her fingers pointed inwards, she tipped her elbow upwards and down again. Her hand stayed flat as it came round, and the stone didn't fall off.

'How do you do it?' gasped Kate, clapping her hands.

'I've been practising,' said Kamla. My cousin Leela showed me how. She can do it with a saucer! I think I'll try that when I get home.'

Kate found herself practising too. She couldn't stop trying to do it. She practised and practised until her muscles ached and she felt as if her arm would drop out of its socket. At last she managed it with a stone. She did it in the playground, and was so pleased that she rushed around shouting, 'I've done it! I've done it!'

She showed Miss Evans, the playground supervisor.

'Aren't you clever,' said Miss Evans and she tried too. It was catching!

'Kamla can do it with a saucer now,' said Kate.

'That could work out expensive,' laughed Miss Evans as she dropped the stone.

The next morning the postman called at Kate's house with a large white envelope. Her dad opened it.

'It's an invitation,' he said. 'We're all invited to a Diwali party at the Guptas next Saturday evening.'

'What's Diwali?' asked Kate's mum.

'It's a Festival of Light, according to one of my mates at work,' said her dad. 'He mentioned it the other day. It should be interesting.'

Kate was very excited. She had never been to an evening party before with grown-ups.

'We're all coming to your party next Saturday,' she told Kamla when she got to school.

'Oh good,' said Kamla. She seemed very excited too, but also a bit secretive.

'We're preparing a lot of surprises for you,' she whispered darkly.

At last Saturday came round. It was a dull, rainy, day. Kate looked gloomily out of the window. How was she going to pass the hours?

'Mum, can I put on my party dress now?' she asked.

'No, dear,' replied her mother. 'It's only nine o'clock in the morning and the party isn't until seven tonight!'

Kate sighed with boredom. Kamla couldn't come round and play because she was helping to prepare the Diwali party.

'Can't I help too?' Kate had asked.

'Oh, no!' cried Kamla. 'You'd find out all the surprises!'

Kate decided to try balancing a saucer on her hand and twisting it round. She twisted carefully ... up ... round ... in ... and CRASH! The saucer slipped from her palm and smashed on the floor.

'What are you doing?' cried her mother rushing in.

'I was practising,' said Kate glumly.

'Not with my saucers, you don't,' retorted her mother. 'Come on, I think you'd better go

101

shopping with Daddy before you get up to any more mischief!'

And so the hours dragged by. But at last darkness fell, and her mother suddenly said, 'Come on Kate! It's time to get ready for the party!'

Kate whooped with joy and rushed up-stairs. There lying on her bed was her long, green and white party dress with frilly sleeves and a green, velvet sash.

Her mother dressed up too in her prettiest skirt and blouse, and her father wore a tie; something he hardly ever did except for wed-dings and funerals! Then they all set off.

It was no longer raining. The night sky had cleared and was spangled with stars. Then they saw the first surprise.

'Look! Look at Kamla's house!' squealed Kate. 'It's all lit up!'

'They're real flames!' exclaimed Mum.

As they drew nearer they could see that every window sill was lined with small saucers of glowing lights. Even the garden path was lined with flickering flames from wicks dipped in oil.

The front door flew open and Kamla came

skipping out. She was wearing her Indian
costume, the pink, satin pyjamas and tunic
which her cousin Leela had brought her from
India.

'Hello! Hello! Come in!' she called excitedly, and she grabbed Kate's hand and pulled
her inside.

'Welcome to our Diwali celebrations,' said
Kamla's mother and father. Kamla's mother
looked very beautiful in a purple and gold
saree, while Mr. Gupta wore special wrinkly,

103

white trousers and a black, silk jacket buttoned up to the neck.

'I'm so glad you could come,' he said, and led them into the living room.

The room was already full of friends and neighbours, all dressed up in their party clothes.

Instead of putting on the electric lights, there were little dishes of oil and wicks flickering in every niche and on the mantelpiece. The light from them made the gold and silver threads in the sarees glisten; it made the sequins and beads on Kamla's costume flash and sparkle; it made the jewels in the necklaces and earrings gleam brightly, and it made the shadows on the walls tremble darkly.

Leela passed among the guests carrying trays of drinks and Indian titbits to nibble. In the dining room the table was piled high with all sorts of delicious food. Plates of chappatis and purees, dishes of chutneys and pickles, great bowls of steaming fluffy rice and rich, red curry and several plates full of different kinds of Indian sweets.

'What a feast!' breathed Kate's dad in amazement.

After everyone had eaten and mingled and chatted, Mr. Gupta clapped his hands.

'Now we have some entertainment for you!'

Everyone sat down excitedly on the chairs and sofas and on the floor, leaving a circle in the middle.

Mr. Gupta brought out his accordian and Mrs. Gupta held two, small, brass bells like tiny cymbals, one in each hand.

There was a jangling of ankle bells, and Leela stepped into the middle of the circle. Everyone clapped with delight. She was wearing an Indian dance costume of scarlet and gold. Her bare feet and hands were painted red, and her eyes were outlined in black to make them look larger.

She stamped her jangly feet and Kamla's mother and father began to play. The dance started slowly as Leela twisted her hands and flashed her eyes. Gradually the beat got faster and faster and soon she was spinning round like a brightly coloured top with her costume whirling round her.

The dance ended with a flourish. Everybody cheered and clapped. Kate looked round for Kamla, but she was nowhere to be seen.

'I can't see Kamla!' Kate whispered.

'Shh!' nudged her mother. 'Mrs. Gupta is going to sing.'

When the song was over, Kate suddenly caught sight of her friend. This was a really big surprise. Kamla was dressed up as a dancing girl too. Her eyes were outlined in black; she had a red mark in the middle of her fore-

head, and the palms of her hands were painted red too. There were jangling bells round her ankles and glass bangles tinkled on her wrists.

'Mummy! Look at Kamla!' cried Kate in astonishment.

Everyone looked surprised. Even Kamla's mother and father.

'Kamla has been secretly learning a very special dance for Diwali,' announced Leela, leading her little cousin into the centre of the circle.

There was a rustle of excitement. Kamla's mother beamed with pleasure.

'Kamla will now dance a temple dance in which she offers a gift of light to the god.' Then Leela stepped over to the mantelpiece and took down a very small saucer with a softly burning light. She placed it on the palm of Kamla's outstretched hand.

'So that's what she was practising so secretly,' hissed Kate. 'I hope she doesn't drop it!'

First Kamla stood like a statue with the flame burning in her hand. Then, as the accordian breathed out its tune, and the bells clashed a rhythm, she stamped first one foot then the other. Gradually she began to move round, gliding gracefully so as not to upset the saucer of flame. She swayed this way and that, raising the saucer from one side to the other.

Then came the really hard bit. Kate could hardly bear to look. Kamla began to twist her palm round as she had done in the playground. Would she drop the saucer? Would she get burnt by the flame as it twisted under? No one dared make a sound.

Kamla twisted the saucer on her palm round ... and round ... and round ... while she gradually dropped lower and lower to the ground. At last she was kneeling and brought the saucer in its last circle down to the ground. She placed it like an offering in the middle of the room.

Everyone burst out cheering and clapping. 'Shabash!' they shouted. 'Well done!' What a secret! Kate didn't know, and not even Kamla's mother had known!

Leela was very proud of her pupil. 'I wanted to teach her an Indian dance before I went home,' she said.

Kamla jingled and jangled as she jumped up and down enjoying all the praise.

'I love dancing,' she cried. 'I wish Leela wasn't going home because there'll be no one to teach me.'

'Why don't you come to my ballet class?' suggested Kate.

'What do you do?' asked Kamla, interested.

'Well, you don't wear bells round your ankles or carry saucers. Instead of stamping you run on tiptoe and point your toes – in ballet shoes of course!'

'Don't you dress up?' asked Kamla, whirling her costume. 'I do love dressing up!'

'Only at Christmas, then sometimes we wear tu-tus like real ballerinas!'

'I think you should go with Kate to her ballet classes,' said Leela. 'Then, when you come and visit me in India one day you can entertain us with ballet dancing!'

'Can I come too?' begged Kate.

'Who knows!' laughed Leela. 'Who knows!'

At last the party was over. Everyone thanked Mr. and Mrs. Gupta, and they thanked Leela and Kamla. Then they went out into the night.

It was just beginning to rain a little and the flames in the saucers began to splutter and go out.

'Could we have a party like that?' asked Kate as they hurried home. 'Then I could dance in my tu-tu for everyone.'

'Let's have a party on Bonfire night,' suggested Dad. 'It's Guy Fawkes night in a week or two.'

'I can't promise a feast like the Guptas gave,' laughed Mum, 'but I think I could manage some baked potatoes and sausages, and mugs of hot chocolate.'

'Yes,' agreed Kate enthusiastically. 'That would be fun. We must send out invitations immediately.'

'Please try and wait till tomorrow,' begged her mother. 'It is nearly midnight.'

'Oh all right!' agreed Kate, and hurried off to bed to dream of bonfires and fireworks and dancing with saucers of flame.

Also by Jamila Gavin

THREE INDIAN PRINCESSES

The stories of Savitri, Damayanti and Sita

* Savitri *

Savitri leaves the palace to live with her husband in the jungle. She carries a dark secret. Satyvan will die within a year . . .

* Damayanti *

Everyone wishes to marry Princess Damayanti, even the gods. However, even the gods consent to the virtuous princess's marriage to King Nala . . . that is all except a demon who lays a curse on the couple.

* Sita *

Prince Rama is about to become king when he is banished by his jealous stepmother for 14 years. His wife, the loyal Sita, follows, but this is only the beginning of their suffering . . .

Three vibrant and powerful Indian folk-tales retold with great sensitivity and charm.

A Selected List of Fiction from Mammoth

While every effort is made to keep prices low, it is sometimes necessary to increase prices at short notice. Mammoth Books reserves the right to show new retail prices on covers which may differ from those previously advertised in the text or elsewhere.

The prices shown below were correct at the time of going to press.

☐	7497 0366 0	**Dilly the Dinosaur**	Tony Bradman	£1.99
☐	7497 0021 1	**Dilly and the Tiger**	Tony Bradman	£1.99
☐	7497 0137 4	**Flat Stanley**	Jeff Brown	£1.99
☐	7497 0048 3	**Friends and Brothers**	Dick King-Smith	£1.99
☐	7497 0054 8	**My Naughty Little Sister**	Dorothy Edwards	£1.99
☐	416 86550 X	**Cat Who Wanted to go Home**	Jill Tomlinson	£1.99
☐	7497 0166 8	**The Witch's Big Toe**	Ralph Wright	£1.99
☐	7497 0218 4	**Lucy Jane at the Ballet**	Susan Hampshire	£2.25
☐	416 03212 5	**I Don't Want To!**	Bel Mooney	£1.99
☐	7497 0030 0	**I Can't Find It!**	Bel Mooney	£1.99
☐	7497 0032 7	**The Bear Who Stood on His Head**	W. J. Corbett	£1.99
☐	416 10362 6	**Owl and Billy**	Martin Waddell	£1.75
☐	416 13822 5	**It's Abigail Again**	Moira Miller	£1.75
☐	7497 0031 9	**King Tubbitum and the Little Cook**	Margaret Ryan	£1.99
☐	7497 0041 6	**The Quiet Pirate**	Andrew Matthews	£1.99
☐	7497 0064 5	**Grump and the Hairy Mammoth**	Derek Sampson	£1.99

All these books are available at your bookshop or newsagent, or can be ordered direct from the publisher. Just tick the titles you want and fill in the form below.

Mandarin Paperbacks, Cash Sales Department, PO Box 11, Falmouth, Cornwall TR10 9EN.

Please send cheque or postal order, no currency, for purchase price quoted and allow the following for postage and packing:

UK	80p for the first book, 20p for each additional book ordered to a maximum charge of £2.00.
BFPO	80p for the first book, 20p for each additional book.
Overseas including Eire	£1.50 for the first book, £1.00 for the second and 30p for each additional book thereafter.

NAME (Block letters) ....

ADDRESS ....

....

....